⭐ FIRST FAIRY TALES ⭐

Hansel and Gretel

D0767467

700029078362

For Natalie - *MM*
For Frederick - *PN*

WORCESTERSHIRE COUNTY
COUNCIL

836

Bertrams   15.03.06

£3.99

Ser... reading consultant: Prue Goodwin,
Reading and Language Information Centre,
University of Reading

Orchard Books
96 Leonard Street, London EC2A 4XD
Orchard Books Australia
32/45-51 Huntley Street, Alexandria, NSW 2015
This text was first published in Great Britain in the form
of a gift collection called *First Fairy Tales*,
illustrated by Selina Young, in 1994
This edition first published in Great Britain in hardback in 2002
First paperback publication 2003
Text © Margaret Mayo 2002
Illustrations © Philip Norman 2002
The rights of Margaret Mayo to be identified as the author and
Philip Norman to be identified as the illustrator have been
asserted by them in accordance with the
Copyright, Designs and Patents Act, 1988.
A CIP catalogue record for this book is available from the British Library
ISBN 1 84121 136 2 (hardback)
ISBN 1 84121 148 6 (paperback)
1 3 5 7 9 10 8 6 4 2 (hardback)
5 7 9 10 8 6 4 (paperback)
Printed in Hong Kong, China

✸ FIRST FAIRY TALES ✸
Hansel and Gretel

Margaret Mayo ✸ Philip Norman

ORCHARD BOOKS

Once upon a time a boy and girl
called Hansel and Gretel lived
with their father and stepmother
in a little house beside a big forest.

The family was very poor and
never had enough to eat.

One night, when the children were in bed, their stepmother said, "Let's take Hansel and Gretel into the forest and leave them there."

"Oh, no! I won't do that," said their father. "I love my children!"

"We must," she said. "We haven't enough food for all of us."

Now, Hansel and Gretel were
so hungry, they couldn't sleep,
and they heard everything.

Gretel began to cry. But Hansel
whispered, "Don't cry, little sister.
I'll look after you!"

Then he crept outside and filled
his pockets with white pebbles.

In the morning, the children's
stepmother told them that the
whole family was going into the
forest to collect firewood.

Off they went. But Hansel
walked behind and dropped white
pebbles on the path.

When they came to a clearing,
the stepmother said, "Wait here
while we chop down some trees."

Now, Hansel and Gretel were
tired and soon fell asleep. When
they woke, it was night.

But, Hansel saw his white
pebbles shining in the moonlight!

So he held Gretel's hand, and
they followed the pebbles back to
their own little house.

Their father was very happy when he saw them, but their stepmother was not.

The next night she said to him, "We must take Hansel and Gretel into the forest again, and this time they must not come back!"

Once again, the children heard everything, and Hansel crept off to find pebbles.

But the door was locked, and he could not get out.

For breakfast their stepmother gave them a piece of dry bread. Hansel put it in his pocket.

Then, the family went off to collect firewood. But Hansel walked behind and dropped white breadcrumbs on the path.

When they were deep in the forest, the stepmother said, "Wait here, while we chop down some trees."

Once again, Hansel and Gretel fell asleep, and when they woke, it was night.

But, Hansel could not see his breadcrumbs. Birds had eaten them.

Hansel did not know which way to go, but he held Gretel's hand, and they walked...and walked.

The next day, they came to a
clearing...and there was a house,
a strange and wonderful house!
It had gingerbread walls, barley-
sugar windows, and a roof made
of cakes and cookies.

16

Hansel snapped off some icing
and bit into it.

Gretel broke off some gingerbread
and popped it in her mouth.

The door opened, and an old woman with ruby-red eyes came out. She said, "Who is nibbling at my house?"

"I'm sorry," said Hansel, "but we're very hungry."

"Then come in," said the
old woman.

So Hansel and Gretel went
in, and she gave them sugary
pancakes, milk and apples.

19

When they had eaten, she took
them into a room with two little
beds, and soon Hansel and Gretel
were fast asleep.

They did not know that the old
woman was a WITCH, who
caught children and ate them!

In the morning, the witch crept in, bent down and looked at the children very closely, because she could not see clearly.

"Too thin to eat!" she said.

She shook Hansel and woke
him...

and she put him in a cage.

She shook Gretel and shouted,
"Get up, lazy-bones! Light the
fire! Wash the dishes! And be
quick about it!"

From that time on, Gretel had
to work hard. But Hansel was
kept in the cage.

The witch gave him lots of food
to make him fat, and every day
she said, "Show me your finger so
I can feel how fat you are."

Now, Hansel had found a small chicken bone in the cage and... *guess what he did.* He pushed out the bone instead of his finger!

When the witch felt the bone, she always said, "Still too thin!"

But one day the witch said to Gretel, "Light the fire and heat the oven. Today I am going to roast your brother and eat him!"

When the oven was very hot, the witch said, "Climb inside and see if it is hot enough."

Gretel said, "How can I get in?"

"Put in your head like this,"
said the witch, leaning forward.

Then Gretel gave her a hard
push, and the witch went head
over heels into the oven.

Gretel slammed the door shut,
and that was the end of the
wicked witch.

Gretel ran to the cage.

She unlocked it, and Hansel was free!

Then they opened the witch's treasure chest and filled their pockets with gold, silver and jewels.

"Let's go home," said Hansel.
They walked...and walked,
until at last they came to a path
they knew. They saw their own
little house, and they ran!

Their father was very happy to
see them. He had looked for them
in the forest every day. This had
made their stepmother angry and
one day she had packed her
clothes and left.

From that time on Hansel,
Gretel and their father lived
happily in the little house beside
the big forest.

Because of the witch's treasure,
they had plenty of money and
could buy lots of food.

So Hansel and Gretel never again went to bed feeling hungry!

FIRST FAIRY TALES

by Margaret Mayo

Illustrated by Philip Norman

Enjoy a little more magic with these First Fairy Tales:

❏ Cinderella	1 84121 150 8	£3.99
❏ Hansel and Gretel	1 84121 148 6	£3.99
❏ Jack and the Beanstalk	1 84121 146 X	£3.99
❏ Sleeping Beauty	1 84121 144 3	£3.99
❏ Rumpelstiltskin	1 84121 152 4	£3.99
❏ Snow White	1 84121 154 0	£3.99

Colour Crackers

by Rose Impey

Illustrated by Shoo Rayner

Have you read any Colour Crackers?

❏ A Birthday for Bluebell	1 84121 228 8	£3.99
❏ Hot Dog Harris	1 84121 232 6	£3.99
❏ Tiny Tim	1 84121 240 7	£3.99
❏ Too Many Babies	1 84121 242 3	£3.99

and many other titles.

First Fairy Tales and Colour Crackers are available from all good
bookshops, or can be ordered direct from the publisher:
Orchard Books, PO BOX 29, Douglas IM99 1BQ
Credit card orders please telephone 01624 836000
or fax 01624 837033
or e-mail: bookshop@enterprise.net for details.

To order please quote title, author and ISBN
and your full name and address.
Cheques and postal orders should be
made payable to 'Bookpost plc'.
Postage and packing is FREE within the UK
(overseas customers should add £1.00 per book).

Prices and availability are subject to change.